Donna Harvey
Old Cooper Road - Alexander
P.O. Box 847
Woodland, ME 04694

A Giant First-Start Reader

This easy reader contains only 48 different words, repeated often to help the young reader develop word recognition and interest in reading.

Basic word list for *Secret Valentine*

a	house	secret
am	I	see
any	is	she
are	it	something
at	me	special
be	Molly	that
but	mouse	there
can	more	to
day	my	valentine
ding-dong	no	valentine's
Dolly	not	Wally
find	Olly	what
friend	one	who
from	out	will
goes	Polly	yes
happy	says	you

Secret Valentine

Written by Laura Damon

Illustrated by Anne Kennedy

Troll Associates

Library of Congress Cataloging in Publication Data

Damon, Laura.
     Secret valentine.

     (A Giant first-start reader)
     Summary: Molly the mouse sets out to find the
identity of the secret friend who sent her a valentine.
     [1. Valentine's Day—Fiction.   2. Mice—Fiction.
3. Animals—Fiction]   I. Kennedy, Anne, 1955-   , ill.
II. Title.   III. Series.
PZ7.D186Se   1988   [E]   87-13736
ISBN 0-8167-1101-1 (lib. bdg.)
ISBN 0-8167-1102-X (pbk.)

10 9 8 7 6 5 4 3

Copyright © 1988 by Troll Associates

Ding-dong.
Who is there?

Ding-dong.

"Who is there?" says Molly Mouse.

Molly goes to see.

Who is there?
No one!
No one is there.

But *something* is there—
a special valentine.

"What a special valentine,"
says Molly.
It is from a secret friend. Who?

Who is that secret friend?
"I will find out," says Molly.

There goes Molly.

She goes to see Olly.

"Are you a secret friend?" says Molly.
"No," says Olly. "I am a friend.
But I am not a secret friend."

There goes Molly.

She goes to see Polly.

"Are you a secret friend?" says Molly.
"No," says Polly. "I am a friend.
But I am not a secret friend."

There goes Molly.

She goes to see Dolly.

"Are you a secret friend?" says Molly.
"No," says Dolly. "I am a friend.
But I am not a secret friend."

"Who is that secret friend?" says Molly.
"Who can it be?"

There goes Molly.
She goes to see Wally.

Ding-dong.
Who is there?

Wally goes to see.

It is Molly!
"Are you a secret friend?" says Molly.

"Yes," says Wally.
"But I am not a secret friend any more!"

Happy Valentine's Day, Molly!
Happy Valentine's Day, Wally!
Happy Valentine's Day to you!